Oscar the Osprey

THE BIRD WHO WAS AFRAID OF HEIGHTS

EDWARD MARTIN POLANSKY

Illustrated by Jean Rosow

authorHOUSE®

AuthorHouse™
1663 Liberty Drive
Bloomington, IN 47403
www.authorhouse.com
Phone: 1 (800) 839-8640

Published by AuthorHouse   05/20/2015

ISBN: 978-1-5049-1010-1 (sc)
ISBN: 978-1-5049-1009-5 (e)

Library of Congress Control Number: 2015906977

Print information available on the last page.

DEDICATION

*T*he inspiration for this book came during a family summer vacation in Wyoming and Colorado. It was a lengthy road trip that included stops in Yellowstone National Park, the Grand Tetons, and the Royal Gorge Park--- all of which played a part in the origins of this book. The source for the story about an acrophobic bird came about as I, along with my family, walked across the suspension bridge spanning the Royal Gorge approximately 1000 feet above the Arkansas River. My oldest son, feeling quite queasy about the heights, exclaimed "It would really suck, if you were a bird and afraid of heights!" That triggered an immediate response in my brain and inspired me to investigate a children's story about overcoming hurdles in life. As the tale evolved, I received many good suggestions from my family for such things as the story's locale, the osprey protagonist, and other animals observed on the trip. I dedicate this book to my dear wife, Helenan, and my two great sons, Charles and Josh, in memory of one of those special times we spent together.

INTRODUCTION

A long time ago, a very interesting thing happened to an osprey who lived near Jenny Lake, which is now part of Grand Teton National Park. The lake was, and still is, a favorite nesting place of ospreys. An osprey is both beautiful and graceful, and it is often called a "fish hawk" because of its love of eating fish. It also looks like a hawk, although smaller, with its hooked beak and its large talons. Our tale is about one special osprey. He tells the story himself.

SPRING

A glint of light flashed in the corner of my eye. I turned and was startled by a creature only a few inches away from my face. It was a butterfly, and the sun was shining through his brightly colored wings. He had landed on the edge of the nest and was fanning his wings to dry them in the warmth of the afternoon sunshine.

His colors were so vibrant; I could not keep my eyes off of him. I wondered if I could catch him. I slowly moved closer, trying not to disturb him.

I hopped up onto the side of the nest. I had never done that before. I was excited, and my heart began to beat rapidly, but as I hopped, the butterfly flitted onto a branch next to the nest. *Oh, I might lose him!* I thought. I moved quickly toward the edge of the nest. He didn't know I was so close. I could almost snatch him with my beak. I eased closer, right to the edge of the nest! I knew I could catch him if I lunged.

Suddenly the whole valley below filled my eyes—and then it happened.

A woozy feeling came over me. I began to lose my balance, and I started to fall forward. The ground far below seemed to be pulling me right out of the nest. Mom screeched, "Oscar!" Then everything went black.

The next thing I remember was lying on my back and looking up at the anguished faces of Mom and Dad. "Are you all right? You almost fell out of the nest! What were you trying to do?" Mom rattled on, obviously very agitated.

Dad's expression slowly returned to normal. "He's waking now. He's okay. Nothing to worry about. Must have been trying to fly, and he fell down and hit his head." He looked satisfied with that explanation, so he left the matter for Mom.

"You could've been killed. You're not ready to fly yet," she said as she wrapped her wings around me.

"Mom, do ospreys eat butterflies?" was all I could think to say. She did not answer, but she seemed relieved to know that I could speak.

As you can see, something strange happened that day to make me faint. It wasn't the last time it happened, either. But let me start my story from the beginning.

My name is Oscar. I was born on a bright, sunny spring day. I remember because the sunlight was so bright it hurt my eyes. In fact, it took a while before I could see anything without squinting. The first thing I saw was my Mom; she seemed so happy. Then I saw my brother and sister, who were not happy at all. My sister, Oprah, and my brother, Otto, were born before me on the same day, and they were already squabbling.

It wasn't a coincidence that we all had names that began with the letter "O." As you might guess, it was the ospreys' favorite letter to use to begin names of newly-hatched chicks. At one time, almost all ospreys had names that began with the letter "O." This made it very confusing for the flock.

So, many generations ago, the elders held a council to discuss the problem. They decided that letters would be assigned each spring by lot. I was told that Mom was overjoyed when she heard that she would get the "O" letter. She said no one in her family had ever had that letter assigned to them before. But Mom and Dad did not see eye-to-eye on this matter.

"This could be a good omen for us," Mom told Dad. "Our offspring will be something special. Their 'O' names must be chosen wisely."

"Actually, I was hoping to name one after Uncle Zonk," Dad said.

"Over my dead body!" exclaimed Mom, flapping her wings wildly, feathers flying in all directions.

Dad was a tough old bird, but he finally gave in to Mom's wishes. My sister, Oprah, was named after the fawn, to represent the animals in the woods. My brother was named Otto after the majestic mountains surrounding the lake where we lived. I guess when I came, Mom got a little carried away, because she named me Oscar, meaning a fearless warrior. I quickly failed to live up to this hero's name.

At first, I thought it was just sibling rivalry that kept me from getting enough to eat. In fact, it took me awhile to realize that Otto and Oprah always got more food than I did. While my stomach growled constantly, they were contentedly stuffed most of the time. Of course, they never let on to Mom.

"Who's the hungriest?" Mom would ask.

"I'm so hungry, I could eat a bison's ear!" Otto would respond, with a desperate look in his eyes.

"Mom, I am famished!" Oprah would say politely while she kicked me out of the way.

I don't know why Mom asked, because she couldn't really be sure how the food was distributed. No matter how hard Mom tried to bring order to the chaos, there was always a feeding fracas. It was strictly first come, first served. And it always seemed that Otto came first, and then Oprah … and then I got the leftovers.

I finally saw what was happening. When Mom arrived with fish from the lake, she hovered above the nest. Otto and Oprah would lean out and battle each other for the fish. That's how they got the food first. *I could do that!* So, the next time Mom came back, I was ready. As I leaned out of the nest, I looked down, Suddenly, I got dizzy. My stomach rose up into my throat, my eyes glazed over—and I blacked out!

That was the second time it happened. But it became a regular occurrence … and a great opportunity for ridicule. By about the twentieth time, I finally learned something.

As I woke up that time, I heard Oprah say, "Mom, Oscar's fainted again!"

Mom, looking off into the sky, sighed. "Whatever am I going to do with that boy?"

"He'd be better off being raised by ground squirrels," Otto teased.

That's when it dawned on me. I had a real problem. I was afraid of heights. I just couldn't climb out on the edge. I decided to just stay put until my problem went away. *It can't last forever,* I thought. And fortunately, enough leftovers fell to the bottom of the nest for me to survive those early days.

But it wasn't long before I learned of another hurdle. Mom told us that our flight training would soon begin. We were to leave the nest and go out onto the limb to begin stretching our wings. Otto and Oprah were anxious to leave the nest, but Mom had to really coax me.

"You'll love the bird's-eye view from out there," she said.

"Can't I just see it from here?" I asked, ducking down below the edge of the nest. I didn't like staying down there though, because it was so cramped. I felt closed in, like I had no room to breathe. So I peeked out from time to time.

It not only bothered me to think about going out on the limb; it bothered me to watch Oprah and Otto do it. I would get a tingling sensation inside my chest long before I ever took a step out of the nest. I was afraid to go out. Mom was patient, but Dad didn't understand my true feelings.

"Oscar, you get your little tail out here this instant or I'll wring your neck!" Dad demanded.

"Now, Oscar, you will be safe with me here," Mom assured me. "Look what I have for you!" She tried tempting me with a piece of fresh fish.

Since I was afraid of what Dad might do and I realized I was a little hungry, I slowly came out of the nest like a worm inching out of its hole. My claws gripped the tree limb so tightly I could barely get them loose to take another step. My heart was beating so hard I couldn't catch my breath.

"Aaaaaaaaaaaaah!" was all that came out of my mouth.

Mom was there to help. She calmed me down with her soft voice. Then it wasn't so bad. I was even beginning to feel that maybe I could overcome my nervousness. I had a plan: I just wouldn't look down. Instead, I'd look straight ahead or up. I even dared to stretch my wings, and it felt wonderful.

The rivalry with Otto and Oprah continued though.

Otto boasted, "See, my wings are so much bigger than yours."

"But mine are prettier," Oprah said as she pranced around the nest.

I was puzzled. "Yeah, but what are they for?" I asked.

"They are for flying and soaring and diving! Just like Dad and I do. You'll learn to fly when you leave the nest today," Mom explained, looking at Dad at the same time. I could see that he was losing his patience. Funny; I never thought my wings were anything more than a place to stick feathers.

When her words sank in, my heart skipped a beat. *Leave the nest … today?* I saw Otto and Oprah lift off from the limb and float away, with Mom close behind. "Come," she yelled, looking back at me. Dad was still impatient and a little bit angry. Without saying much he gave me a gentle push, and I was off into the morning mist. It wasn't too bad, until I made my mistake—I looked down!

"Ooooooooooooooooooh!"

Ker-plunk! I had spiraled face down into a pile of dried pine needles.

kah-plunk!

I couldn't move. Every bone in my body hurt; even my feathers seemed to ache. I saw Otto and Oprah swooping around—way up, then way down, right by my head. There was sheer delight in their eyes and voices as they flew, free as birds. *Swoosh* they went, hurling insults as they passed by.

"How do pine needles taste?" Otto yelled.

"Oscar, the warrior of the sky, is grounded!" Oprah said.

I was embarrassed. Ospreys from everywhere rushed to see what had happened. I wanted to hide, but I shook the pine needles out of my beak and feathers and stretched my wings. Nothing was broken. I flapped my wings and began to rise. It felt all right. I was flying! I might even catch up with Otto and Oprah. *They might accept me yet.* But then I looked down again.

"Ooooooooooooooh!"

Ker-plunk! I crashed again, this time on some bison droppings. I wanted to disappear, to get away from all the other ospreys who were watching me and chirping at my failures.

Mom had faith in me. Calmly, she encouraged me to keep trying. I did, again and again, but every time I got above a certain height, I became dizzy, my underwings would sweat, my heart would flutter, and I would lose control and fall. As much as I wanted to be with Otto and Oprah and the other ospreys, I just couldn't fly that high.

How humiliating! Mom always had to come and get me and carry me like a fish back to the nest. Otto and Oprah were becoming embarrassed; imagine having a brother who couldn't fly!

But Mom didn't give up. Every day she would take me to the ground, and I tried to fly up from there. Otto and Oprah would leave the nest early so they wouldn't be around when the other ospreys saw Mom carry me down.

Dad did not approve at all.

"If you don't stop doing everything for Oscar, he will not be able to survive," Dad said sternly.

"Just give him a little while longer; he'll make it," Mom said. "I promise."

"You mean, if he doesn't die of embarrassment first," Dad muttered under his breath.

But eventually I did learn to fly. Just not too high. I became an expert at low-level flying, and although there were certain hazards of flying so low—like skinning your claws—I developed some unusual skills. For example, while all the other ospreys would fish from high up by making long dives, talons outstretched, and splashing almost out of sight in a large spray of water, I skimmed the surface at a high speed, catching fish that would otherwise escape. In fact, I spent most of my time perfecting this technique, since I really didn't have any friends to keep me company anyway.

SUMMER

*A*s the days passed and grew warmer, it became clearer to me that I wasn't outgrowing my disability. I tried everything that Mom or I could think of to overcome my problem.

I tried flying while only looking straight up, and I nearly broke my lower beak on a lodge-pole pine tree. I flew with my eyes closed and accidentally bumped heads with a surprised and angry Otto. I even tried flying in a fog, and that time I went flying high with no serious side effects—except for the side of the mountain I crashed into.

I did, however, get better and better at scooping up fish in the lake, and my low-flying technique did not go unnoticed. Although the other ospreys made fun of my strange methods, they watched with curiosity. They soon discovered that I caught more fish than they did. However, I had a dilemma. I could only get my catch to shore: getting it up to the nest required flying high. As a result, all the other young ospreys began to wait on shore to take my catch. This caused a crisis within the Elder Council, and they came to talk to Mom and Dad. I hid behind some tree limbs to listen to what the Elders had to say.

As they approached Mom and Dad, I could tell which ones were the most important Elders by their pecking order. Spreading his wings, the leader spoke first with a booming voice, startling my folks.

"Something needs to be done about Oscar," he said. "He is ruining the other younger ospreys because they are doing less dive-fishing and are now waiting on shore to steal Oscar's catch. Oscar is becoming a bad influence."

"We will tell Oscar not to skim-fish anymore." Dad cowered, having never had an Elder, much less the leader of the council, address him directly before.

Mom added, "He will do what he is told—"

"See that he does!" said the leader.

So I was told not to skim-fish anymore. Nothing seemed to be working out in my life. Secretly, I did my fishing in the early morning hours before the adult ospreys came out. It wasn't as good, but I did eat.

I also did a lot of walking. If none of the ospreys wanted to hang around with me, at least I could visit with the other animals in the forest. It didn't matter to them that I couldn't fly high. As a matter of fact, most of the animals had never met an osprey before and were very happy to talk with me.

They told me stories of winter. I didn't understand anything they talked about, especially something they called white flaky rain that fell on the ground, covering everything. It was pleasant but unimportant talk to me.

One day I came across a moose that was drinking from one of the ponds. Normally, moose were unfriendly because all they seemed to care about was eating. This one told me that's how they survived.

"We eat as much as possible before the winter comes, because there is very little to eat in the winter," he explained.

"You mean you moose don't ever enjoy yourselves, never stop to smell the roses?"

"Only the ones we eat!"

He did take time that day, though, to tell me of trails that led up the mountains surrounding the lake. I began exploring the trails. I often followed those leading way up the side of the mountains to view the other ospreys eye-to-eye. I would stay way back from the edge, of course, because heights still made me nervous. I had fantasies of jumping off and soaring with the other young ospreys. In reality, they just teased me.

"Come on, land-lover, come fly with us," the ospreys would say, wings flapping in unison and blowing dust in my face. They did this because they knew dust always made me sneeze.

When they teased me, I would approach the edge, and even peer over. My heart would say "Go!" but my stomach would churn a big "No!" inside. The valley and lake seemed so far below; I just couldn't do it. So it was another long walk back. I was the only osprey in the flock with sore feet … and hay fever.

AUTUMN

One day after I came down from the mountain, Mom took me aside so no one else could hear her. She quietly told me that all the ospreys were going to fly south for the winter, and would have to fly over many mountains on the journey. She asked me if I could fly with the others yet.

"Why do we have to fly somewhere else? We have everything we need right here," I said.

"No bird can survive the winter beside this lake. We will come back in the spring." She said the lake would be frozen over—whatever that meant. "Oscar, you must be ready when the Elders say it is time to go."

For several days, I thought about what she said. I tried again.

"Ooooooooooooh!"

Ker-plunk! Luckily, this time I fell onto something soft and damp from the recent rainfall. As I dried myself in the sun, Oprah landed beside me.

"Maybe I could walk over the mountains," I told Oprah.

"Not unless you wear snowshoes!" She laughed, but I did not get the joke.

Oprah, you oaf! I wanted to say, but I couldn't. I just stared at her as she flew back to the flock. She was no help.

The evenings were colder now, and the other birds grew restless. Excitement filled the air, like when a dangerous animal was near. I even felt something swelling up inside of me, like a stomach-ache. I told Mom about how I felt, and she said it meant it was time to go.

"No osprey can survive the winter here; we must go where it is warmer."

"But other animals can't fly, and they remain here. Why can't we?"

"They have coats of fur to keep them warm. We don't," she replied. All I could think of was how I could quickly get a coat of fur.

The flock began to leave the next morning. One after another they took off: first the Elders, then the younger ones following behind, trying to keep as close as possible so they wouldn't lose their way.

Finally, the only ones left were Mom and me. She looked up to watch the last of the others leave. Then she began to rise, calling to me to follow.

Her last words—as if by some miracle I would follow later—were that they would travel with the sun rising on the left and setting on the right. At night they would be guided by the star that doesn't move in the sky. I'm sure I saw tears in her eyes when she left.

I tried to fly one more time.

"Oooooooooooooooooh!"

Ker-plunk! I fell on a hard rock by the lake. I said a word that my mom would have scratched me for saying, if she had heard it. I pecked at the bruise on my ankle. Then I looked up. I was alone. For the first time in my life, I felt a cold chill. *Where can I find a coat of fur?*

For several days I streaked low over the water, scooping all the fish out of the lake that I could possibly eat. I gorged myself because there were no other birds to take my catch now. I began to think that this might not be so bad. After all, Mom said they would be back after the winter. I might even enjoy a little peace for a while, free from the insults of the other ospreys and the stares of the Elders.

It was getting colder, but that was no problem for me. There was plenty of nesting material around to build a cozy, comfortable nest. Things seemed to be finally working out all right. Or so I thought.

WINTER

One morning as I flew along the lake, expecting to catch my first meal of the day, I was stunned when I almost knocked my beak off on the hard surface of the water. It was frozen! *That's what Mom was talking about.*

I could actually walk on water. I could see the fish beneath the hard surface, but I could not get to them.

For a few days I was fine. Then my hunger started to worry me. I began to think I could eat a bison's ear, as Otto had bragged. After some effort, I discovered I could get water to drink, but I had to fly way out to the middle of the lake, where it wasn't frozen. However, I could only get into the water for a short while each time to catch fish, because it was so cold. *Will the whole lake be frozen someday?*

Every day it became harder to warm up from the journeys outside of my nest. Even the nest was getting colder, and the winds were getting stronger. Luckily, I had made my nest in the lower branches of a pine tree, almost a bird's nest on the ground. I had no trouble flying up to it, and it was out of the direct wind.

Fewer animals were out now. One day I came upon a ground squirrel scurrying around, and he took time to talk to me.

"What are you still doing here?" he asked, surprised to see me.

"I've decided to spend the winter on the lake," I said, trying to act as though it was my own idea.

"You will die!" he said. "No bird can last out in the cold." He thought for a moment. "You can share my hole if you like."

I thanked him but declined. I knew I could not go into his hole, because I was afraid of closed-in places.

The next day I met a black bear who was sluggishly walking down a trail. I usually avoided bears; you never knew when they were going to be in a bad mood. But this one wasn't very frightening, and I needed to ask him a question. He seemed to be preoccupied with his own thoughts and was startled to see a bird standing next to him.

"Hello, little fellow! You'd better be going before the winter storms come," he said.

"Do you know where I can get a fur coat for the winter?" I asked.

"I must be getting very tired, because I'm dreaming," he muttered and turned to go on his way.

"No, wait, I need to find a coat!"

"Hah!" he said with a big belly laugh that seemed to wake him up. "So you want to be a bird of a different feather?"

He explained that for me to have a fur coat, some animal would have to give up his own protection from the cold. I thought about that and decided I could not make any animal go naked in the winter; that would not do at all. "What else can I do?" I asked.

Although he yawned a lot during our talk, he explained how he slept through the whole winter. However, I never stayed asleep more than a few minutes at a time. As he wearily trudged off, he said he just had to get to his den before he fell asleep on the trail.

As the sun set that night, white flaky rain started to come down. It was snow! It was very pretty, and by morning it covered everything just the way the animals had described. It continued snowing for several days. I couldn't leave my nest while it fell, because I couldn't see trails or other landmarks I normally used to get my bearings. When the sun finally came out, everything glittered. The world was so bright I could hardly see. I felt as if the sun was coming from all directions. It was a blustery day, and the wind whistled through the nest, which swayed back and forth with the tree.

"Grrrrrrrrrrrrrrrrr." The sound sent a chill up my back. *Was that the wind?* I looked over the side of the nest. All I saw were paw prints in the snow. They were all around the tree. Then I saw him, staring straight at me with his great big gaping mouth, the glare of the sun flashing off his pointed white teeth. *A timber wolf!*

He growled again, coughed, and said, "You look cold, little osprey. Why don't you come down here and let me warm you up?" He had his front paws on the tree trunk, stretching to reach my nest. There was a hungry look in his eyes, like the one Otto used to have before Mom brought food.

"No, I'm warm where I am, thank you," I said timidly. I began to shiver, not sure whether it was from the wind and cold, my lack of food, or fright. I felt the wolf sensed fear. He dropped down and circled the tree again.

"Why are you still here?" he asked. Without waiting for my reply, he said, "If you are hurt, I can help. I know a place where you'll be just fine." I knew where he was talking about—his stomach! I wished I hadn't moved my nest down so low in the tree. Still, I didn't think he could reach me.

29

He moved away from the tree. Then he ran and jumped up, brushing his nose on the bottom of the nest. He tried again. This time he took some of the twigs from the nest with his teeth. He seemed to be getting more frantic, coming closer each time he jumped. Finally, with one jump, he ripped a hole in the bottom of the nest that was big enough for me to see through. I felt a cold breeze whip through the hole.

"Grrrrrrrrrrrrrrrrr." I heard the sound from another direction. I couldn't see very far because of the sunlight reflecting off the snow. Just then, two more wolves walked into the shadow of the tree and met the first wolf.

I could hear them arguing about me. "He must be hurt." "I saw him first; he's mine!" It was clear to me that they were not discussing my warmth or well-being. They began growling and showing their fangs to each other.

I decided it would not be long before they settled their argument and that I had to get out of the nest to find safety and something to eat, no matter how cold it was. I squinted because the light was so strong. I could barely make out shapes in the distance. The sun's brightness hurt my eyes, just like it did on the day I was born.

The wolves now turned away from each other and looked up at me. I sensed they were about to attack. I had to do something. Suddenly, they ran and jumped in unison. I flapped my wings, and as I felt them crash against the nest, I flew away. The wolves glared at me with fire in their eyes and the remains of my nest in their mouths. Then they looked at each other in disgust. Their breakfast had flown the coop.

Out from under the shade of the tree, I was blinded by the brilliant light. I squinted my eyes and flew in a straight line toward the objects I remembered. The wind was blowing so hard that I was barely able to keep a level flight. The swirling winds seemed to blow me in all directions at once.

After flying for a long time, I spied a spot in the distance where I could land. I slowed and softly touched down, feeling my way more than seeing it. There was some shade there, and I opened my eyes wide for the first time since leaving my nest.

"Eek!" I squawked. I was high up on the side of the mountain, higher than I'd ever flown before without fainting.

"That's it!" I said out loud.

By squinting just so, I could fly high, go in the right direction, and not faint. Could I follow the instructions Mom gave me? After checking the sun's direction, I set off in search of the flock, flapping as hard as I could, fighting against the wind, and squinting all the way.

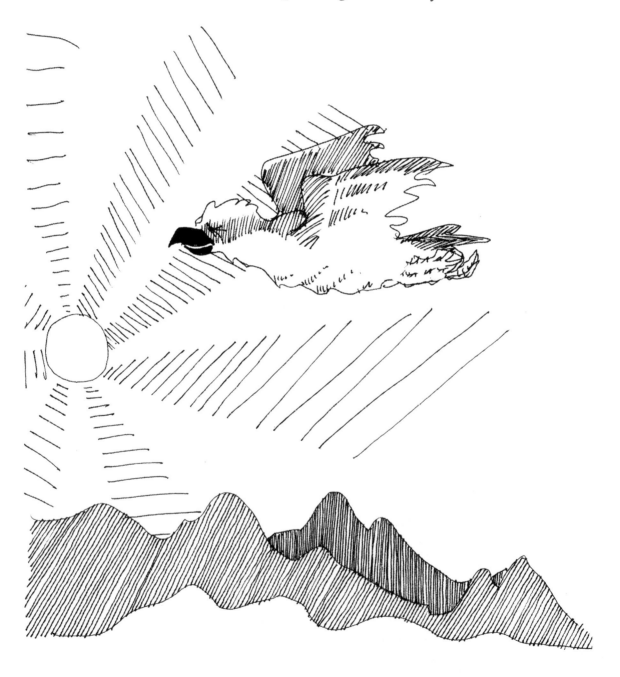

SPRING, AGAIN

I survived the winter, although I never caught up with the flock. My flying was pretty slow. After flying for many days and nights, I found a warmer valley and a pond that had not frozen over. It had plenty of fish—wonderful fish!

In the spring, I was the first one back to the lake. I gleefully greeted the returning ospreys, who were shocked to see me alive. Mom was especially happy to see me.

"Well, it's Oscar. I never … he's alive!" she said, not believing her eyes, wrapping her wings around me. They felt so good.

Dad was speechless. He just stared. But slowly his breast began to swell with pride as he looked around, noticing everyone's amazement—including the Elders—at his son, me! The Elders were huddling together, talking under their breaths with each other. Dad told me later that he overheard the leader say in a low voice, "We should reconsider Oscar; I think we may learn something from him."

Both Otto and Oprah were delighted, particularly when all the others treated me like a hero. I had lived up to my warrior name after all. I was something special now. No one knew of any osprey who had ever survived a winter on his own.

"From now on, Oscar, I'll help you keep the fish you catch!" Otto promised, looking menacingly around at the other young ospreys.

"And I'll prepare your fish to make them taste great," Oprah joyfully added.

All the special attention made me feel uncomfortable, and for a moment I wished to be back by myself. But not really; for the first time in my life I felt like I belonged.

I never could fly above a low level without squinting. I never became anything special above that height, but I did get where I wanted to go. One thing was certain though; at a low level, I was the best there was. They even named the newly-hatched after me that spring—in those families that got the "O" letter, that is.

I planned to be the first to leave when winter came that year. I was pretty slow, you know.

The End ... Maybe

Edward Martin Polansky
Author

Edward Martin Polansky is a Certified Public Accountant in San Antonio and has been in public practice for over forty years with Ernst & Young, with his own firm, and with a regional accounting firm, Weaver and Tidwell LLP. He currently is Of Counsel with Weaver and consults with individuals and businesses on tax and financial planning matters. During his career he has written for various technical publications and lectured on numerous professional topics. *Oscar the Osprey* is his initial effort as an author of a children's book, although he has had an avid interest in children's literature ever since he worked in the children's department of the Corpus Christi Texas Public Library while in high school and college.

Jean Rosow
Illustrator

Jean Rosow interprets objects and scenes around her—from the serene elegance of a tropical courtyard to the subtle details of a passing sailboat. The artist studied at the Art Institute of Chicago and graduated from Northern Illinois University in 1966. Since then she has been making her pen-and-ink sketches and watercolor paintings across the USA, Europe, the Middle East, and the former USSR. Her award-winning works are displayed in galleries, homes, and places of business in many states. Her clients include private individuals, corporations, advertising agencies, municipalities, and non-profit organizations. She lives in San Antonio, Texas, with her husband.

Printed in the United States
By Bookmasters